For:
_____

With love:
_____

LOVE
from Sesame Street

by Sesame Workshop
Illustrated by Ernie Kwiat

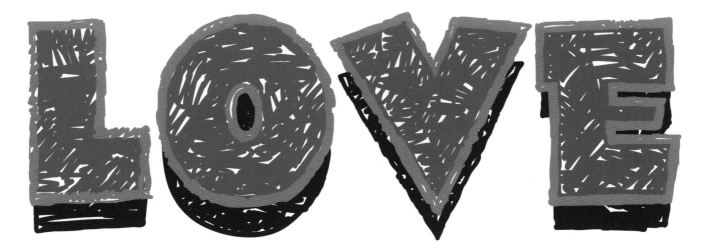

LOVE

IS BEING AN EVERYDAY

HERO.

LOVE IS INFINITE— BIGGER THAN ALL OF THE NUMBERS.

LOVE

comes in all
SHAPES and SIZEs.

LOVE

IS GIGGLES,
AND KISSES, AND HUGS,
AND SQUISHES.

LOVE SINGS IN EVERY LANGUAGE.

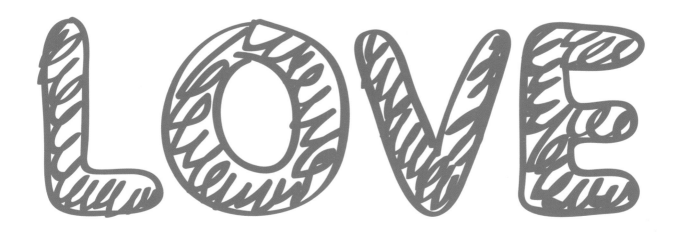

LOVE

is being kind to all
your best friends.

MAKES ALL KINDS OF SOUNDS.

HONK, HONK!

LOVE

IS ACCEPTING
LIFE EVEN WHEN
IT IS MESSY!

  **is**

 **AMAZING FAMILY** and a soft bunny.

is

cookies...

and then
more cookies.

and all around us.

Love

Look and Find

Go back through the book and see if you can find a heart hidden on these pages!

- 💜 **Love is a sunny day!**
  - 💜 **Love is infinite—bigger than all of the numbers.**
  - 💜 Love is being kind to all your best friends.
  - 💜 **Love is accepting life even when it is messy!**
  - 💜 Love is an amazing family and a soft bunny.
  - 💜 Love is everywhere and all around us.

Source of Production: PrintPlus Limited, Shenzhen, Guangdong Province, China • Date of Production: December 2020 • Run Number: 5020466 • Printed and bound in China.
PP 10 9 8 7 6 5 4 3 2